Banana Patch Press
www.bananapatchpress.com

Library of Congress Control number: 2019901471
ISBN-13: 9780980006339

Printed in China

A Mahalo Day!

By Dr. Carolan
& Joanna Carolan

It is not happiness that makes you grateful;
it is gratefulness that makes you happy.
Brother David Steindl-Rast

Mahalo is the Hawaiian word for thanks, gratitude and appreciation.

Teaching gratefulness to your child can give them important lifelong benefits. Studies have shown that grateful people are happier and more optimistic; they are less prone to depression, anxiety and substance abuse. Modeling gratefulness, helping your child to understand gratitude and express appreciation are lifelong gifts you can give your child.

Mahalo to our dear friend, Brother David Steindl-Rast. We have learned so much from Brother David's teachings on gratefulness (gratefulness.org).

Mahalo also to Robert A. Emmons, Ph.D. for his writings and studies on the science of gratitude.

Mahalo nui loa,
Dr. Carolan & Joanna Carolan

For Liam and Keegan

Mahalo is a Hawaiian word.
Mahalo means thank you.
Mahalo is something
You can say, feel, or do!

Mahalo for the sun,
For giving warmth and light.
Mahalo, sun!
For shining so bright!

But what if it is raining outside?
Should I feel sad and blue?
No, instead I can say, Mahalo, rain!
Because rain is important, too.

Mahalo to the rain for
Helping the plants grow.
Mahalo rain, for
Making a rainbow!

On a Mahalo day when I'm hungry,
And Mom dishes up my plate.
I say, Mahalo Mom!
This breakfast looks great!

And on a Mahalo day when Dad
Helps me pack my lunch,
I say, Mahalo Dad!
Thanks a bunch!

When I go to see a friend,
Because it's a Mahalo day,
I say to them, Mahalo,
For having me over to play!

Mahalo for being my friend.
I had fun on our bike ride!
Mahalo, my friend, for
The fun waterslide!

When I go to the beach and
Uncle helps me surf a wave,
I say, Mahalo Uncle!
For helping me be brave!

Mahalo to Papa, for fixing
My snorkel and mask!
Papa saw what I needed,
I didn't even have to ask!

Mahalo to the lifeguards,
For always being there.
Mahalo for the honu
I saw coming up for air.

I'm writing a card to my Tutu
Because she's always so nice.
Mahalo Tutu, for buying me
A rainbow shave ice!

But when it's a Mahalo day
What are you supposed to do
When something happens that
You don't want to happen to you?

I fell down and
My knee really stings.
And my best friend won't
Play with me on the swings.

Something good might happen
Along with something bad.
Something might surprise you
A small thing can help you feel glad.

Mahalo to Auntie, for
Putting a bandaid on my knee.
Mahalo for helping me discover
Swinging is fun – even if it's just me!

It's dinner time and
We're having barbeque!
Mahalo, Mom. Mahalo, Dad.
Mahalo for all you do!

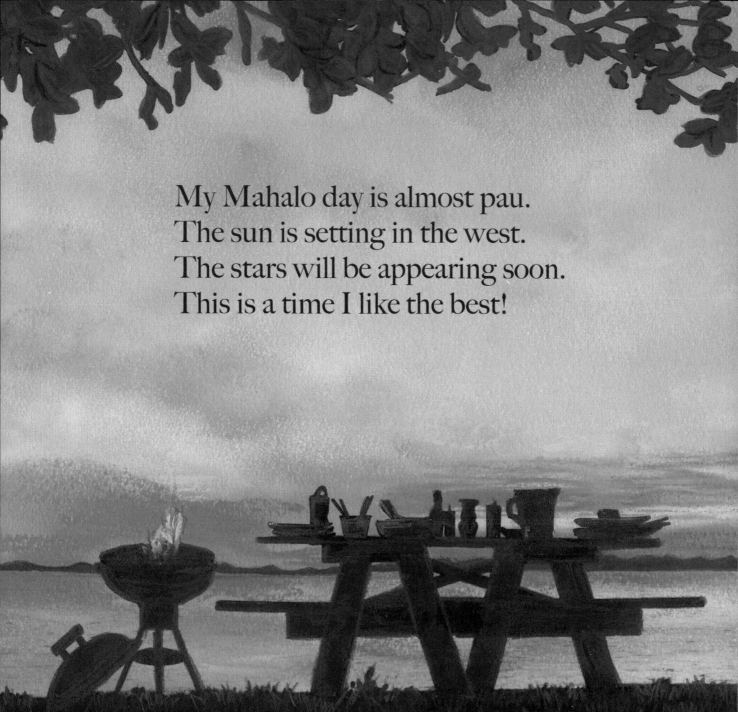

My Mahalo day is almost pau.
The sun is setting in the west.
The stars will be appearing soon.
This is a time I like the best!

Mahalo to the sun,
For painting the sky so bright.
Mahalo, sun! Soon it will be
Time to say goodnight.

Mahalo for my pillow,
So soft under my head.
Mahalo, Dad. Mahalo, Mom.
For tucking me into bed.

I think about all I've seen today,
And everything that made me glad.
This Mahalo day is over now,
But I don't have to feel sad.

Mahalo doesn't have to end.
Because this is what I know:
Every day can be a Mahalo day!
Let's have another one...

Tomorrow!

Dr. Carolan was born in Melbourne, Australia. He moved to Hawaiʻi in 1977. He has been a pediatrician in private practice on the island of Kauaʻi, Hawaiʻi since 1979. He has four sons and six grandchildren.

Joanna F. Carolan was born in San Francisco, California. Her grandparents moved to Kauaʻi in 1967; she spent part of her teenage years living with them in Wailua. She is an artist and owner of Banana Patch Studio and Gallery on Kauaʻi.

Other Dr. Carolan books available from Banana Patch Press:

> Ten Days in Hawaii, A Counting Book
> B is for Beach, An Alphabet Book
> Where are My Slippers? A Book of Colors
> Goodnight Hawaiian Moon
> Old Makana Had A Taro Farm
> This is My Piko
> A President of Hawaiʻi
> The Magic ʻUkulele

For more information visit:
www.bananapatchpress.com www.bananapatchstudio.com